Goats

By JoAnn Early Macken

Reading Consultant: Jeanne Clidas, Ph.D.
Director, Roberts Wesleyan College Literacy Clinic

WEEKLY READER®
PUBLISHING

Please visit our web site at **www.garethstevens.com**.
For a free catalog describing our list of high-quality books,
call 1-877-542-2595 (USA) or 1-800-387-3178 (Canada).
Our fax: 1-877-542-2596

Library of Congress Cataloging-in-Publication Data

Macken, JoAnn Early, 1953–
    Goats / by JoAnn Early Macken.
       p. cm. — (Animals that live on the farm)
    Includes bibliographical references and index.
    ISBN-10: 1-4339-2397-1   ISBN-13: 978-1-4339-2397-5 (lib. bdg.)
    ISBN-10: 1-4339-2466-8   ISBN-13: 978-1-4339-2466-8 (soft cover)
    1. Goats—Juvenile literature. I. Title.
SF383.35.M22 2010
636.3'9—dc22
                                                  2009004176

This edition first published in 2010 by
Weekly Reader® Books
An Imprint of Gareth Stevens Publishing
1 Reader's Digest Road
Pleasantville, NY 10570-7000 USA

Executive Managing Editor: Lisa M. Herrington
Senior Editor: Barbara Bakowski
Project Management: Spooky Cheetah Press
Cover Designers: Jennifer Ryder-Talbot and Studio Montage
Production: Studio Montage
Library Consultant: Carl Harvey, Library Media Specialist, Noblesville, Indiana

Photo credits: Cover, pp. 1, 5, 7, 9, 13, 15 Shutterstock; p. 11 © James P. Rowan; p. 17 © Sharon Eide
and Elizabeth Flynn/SandEphoto.com; pp. 19, 21 Gregg Andersen

Printed in the United States of America

1 2 3 4 5 6 7 8 9 14 13 12 11 10 09

Table of Contents

Boldface words appear in the glossary.

A Different Kind of Kid

A baby goat is called a **kid**.
A kid can stand soon after it
is born.

4

kid

A kid drinks milk from its mother at first. After a few weeks, it eats hay or grain.

Kids play with each other.

They leap and climb.

They wag their short tails.

A goat that is one year old is called a **yearling**.

yearlings

Grown-Up Goats

Male and female goats have horns. Many goats also have beards.

horns

beard

11

In warm weather, goats stay outside. They eat plants, roots, nuts, and berries. They nibble grass. A group of goats is called a **herd**.

herd

In cold or wet weather, goats stay in a barn or shed. They keep out of the rain, snow, and wind.

Work and Play

Some people keep goats as pets. Others use goats to carry loads. A goat may wear a basket over its back or pull a small cart.

Some farmers raise goats for their **wool**. The farmer cuts off the goats' wool so it can be made into yarn.

wool

Some farmers raise goats for milk. They milk the goats twice a day.

Fast Facts

Height	about 3 feet (1 meter) at the shoulder
Length	about 4 feet (1 meter) nose to tail
Weight	about 120 pounds (54 kilograms)
Diet	grass, plants, nuts, roots, and berries
Average life span	up to 15 years

Glossary

herd: a large group of goats or other animals

kid: a baby goat

wool: a goat's coat

yearling: a goat that is one year old

For More Information

Books

Goats. Blastoff Readers: Farm Animals (series). Emily K. Green (Children's Press, 2007)

Goats. Down on the Farm (series). Sally Morgan (Crabtree Publishing, 2008)

Web Sites

Breeds of Goats
www.ansi.okstate.edu/breeds/goats
Read about many kinds of goats.

Kids' Farm: Goats
nationalzoo.si.edu/Animals/KidsFarm/InTheBarn/Goats/factsheet.cfm
Meet the goats at the National Zoo Kids' Farm.

Index

About the Author

JoAnn Early Macken is the author of two rhyming picture books, *Sing-Along Song* and *Cats on Judy*, and more than 80 nonfiction books for children. Her poems have appeared in several children's magazines. She lives in Wisconsin with her husband and their two sons.